OLD DOG BABY BABY

Julie Fogliano art by Chris Raschka

A NEAL PORTER BOOK

ROARING BROOK PRESS
NEW YORK

For Jaxi and Maki
(and their old dog Willy) —*J. F.*

For Neal Porter —*C. R.*

Text copyright © 2016 by Julie Fogliano
Illustrations copyright © 2016 by Chris Raschka
A Neal Porter Book
Published by Roaring Brook Press
Roaring Brook Press is a division of Holtzbrinck Publishing Holdings Limited Partnership
175 Fifth Avenue, New York, New York 10010
Artwork medium: The artwork for this book was created using watercolor on paper.
mackids.com

First edition 2016
Printed in China by Toppan Leefung Printing Ltd., Dongguan City, Guangdong Province.

10 9 8 7 6 5 4 3 2 1

Library of Congress Control Number: 2015042624

ISBN 978-1-59643-853-8

Our books may be purchased in bulk for promotional, educational, or business use.
Please contact your local bookseller or the Macmillan Corporate and Premium Sales Department
at (800) 221-7945 ext. 5442 or by e-mail at MacmillanSpecialMarkets@macmillan.com.

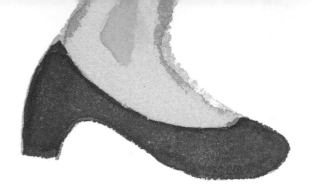

old dog

lazy

lazy

lying on the

kitchen floor

old dog tail
and old dog nose
one eye opened
two eyes closed

old dog dreams
old dog twitches
old paw scratches
old ear itches

old dog
grumble
snorey
sleeping on the
kitchen floor

here comes
baby
baby
crawling through the
kitchen door

baby fingers

baby toes

"puppy! puppy!"

baby goes

baby hurry

baby wiggle

"puppy! puppy!"

baby giggle

here comes
baby
baby
crawling across the
kitchen floor

old dog

stretchy

blinky

waking on the

kitchen floor

old dog sniffs
with old dog nose
baby fingers
baby toes

old dog tongue
old dog floppy
old dog kisses
old dog sloppy

old tail
happy
waggy
thumping on the
kitchen floor

old dog
baby baby
playing on the
kitchen floor

baby poke
baby squeeze
old dog paws
and old dog knees

baby peeks
baby spies
in old dog ears
and old dog eyes

old dog
baby baby

rolling on the
kitchen floor

old dog
baby baby
lying on the
kitchen floor

baby yawn
baby rest
baby head
on old dog chest

old dog yawn

old dog rest

old dog head
on baby chest

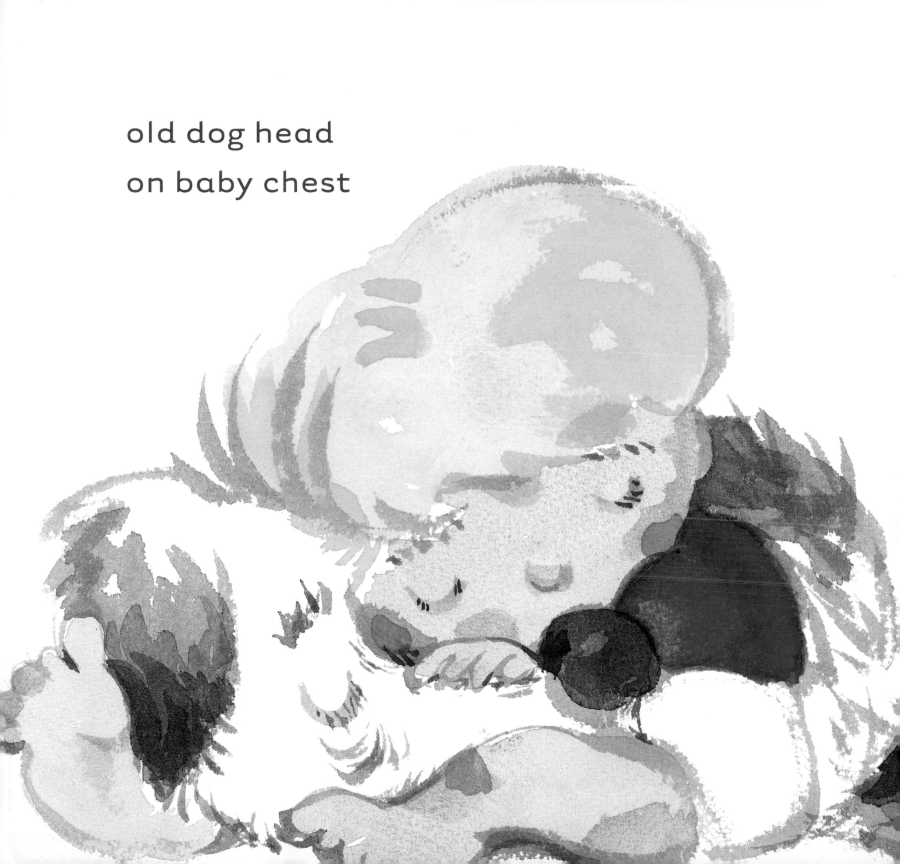

old dog

baby

baby

dreaming on the
kitchen floor